Dear Parents and Educators,

Welcome to Penguin Young Readers! As parents ~~and~~ ~~~~
know that each child develops at his or her own pace—in terms of
speech, critical thinking, and, of course, reading. Penguin Young
Readers recognizes this fact. As a result, each Penguin Young Readers
book is assigned a traditional easy-to-read level (1–4) as well as a
Guided Reading Level (A–P). Both of these systems will help you choose
the right book for your child. Please refer to the back of each book for
specific leveling information. Penguin Young Readers features esteemed
authors and illustrators, stories about favorite characters, fascinating
nonfiction, and more!

Anna Sewell's Black Beauty

LEVEL **4**

GUIDED
READING
LEVEL **N**

This book is perfect for a **Fluent Reader** who:
- can read the text quickly with minimal effort;
- has good comprehension skills;
- can self-correct (can recognize when something doesn't sound right); and
- can read aloud smoothly and with expression.

Here are some **activities** you can do during and after reading this book:
- Discuss: This story is told in the first person—from Black Beauty's point
  of view. How would this story be different if it were told from another
  character's point of view?
- The author uses descriptive words throughout the story: "It was *bitter*
  cold." How many descriptive words can you find in the story?
- Make a list of words and/or pictures from the story that tell you it does
  not take place in present day. For example, a horse-drawn carriage.

Remember, sharing the love of reading with a child is the best gift
you can give!

—Bonnie Bader, EdM, and Katie Carella, EdM
  Penguin Young Readers program

*Penguin Young Readers are leveled by independent reviewers applying the standards developed by Irene Fountas
and Gay Su Pinnell in *Matching Books to Readers: Using Leveled Books in Guided Reading*, Heinemann, 1999.

To Kathy M for sharing her horse expertise
and to those who rescue animals of all kinds
and advocate better treatment for them.
—CW

Penguin Young Readers
Published by the Penguin Group
Penguin Group (USA) Inc., 375 Hudson Street, New York, New York 10014, USA
Penguin Group (Canada), 90 Eglinton Avenue East, Suite 700, Toronto, Ontario M4P 2Y3, Canada
(a division of Pearson Penguin Canada Inc.)
Penguin Books Ltd., 80 Strand, London WC2R 0RL, England
Penguin Group Ireland, 25 St. Stephen's Green, Dublin 2, Ireland
(a division of Penguin Books Ltd.)
Penguin Group (Australia), 250 Camberwell Road, Camberwell, Victoria 3124, Australia
(a division of Pearson Australia Group Pty. Ltd.)
Penguin Books India Pvt. Ltd., 11 Community Centre, Panchsheel Park, New Delhi—110 017, India
Penguin Group (NZ), 67 Apollo Drive, Rosedale, Auckland 0632, New Zealand
(a division of Pearson New Zealand Ltd.)
Penguin Books (South Africa) (Pty.) Ltd., 24 Sturdee Avenue, Rosebank,
Johannesburg 2196, South Africa

Penguin Books Ltd., Registered Offices: 80 Strand, London WC2R 0RL, England

Text copyright © 2009 by Cathy East. Illustrations copyright © 2009 by Christina Wald. All rights
reserved. First published in 2009 by Grosset & Dunlap, an imprint of Penguin Group (USA) Inc.
Published in 2011 by Penguin Young Readers, an imprint of Penguin Group (USA) Inc., 345 Hudson
Street, New York, New York 10014. Manufactured in China.

Library of Congress Control Number: 2008043356

ISBN 978-0-448-45190-9   10 9 8 7 6

PENGUIN YOUNG READERS

LEVEL
FLUENT
READER
4

Anna Sewell's
Black Beauty

adapted by Cathy East
illustrated by Christina Wald

Penguin Young Readers
An Imprint of Penguin Group (USA) Inc.

My name is Black Beauty. The first place I remember was a large, pleasant meadow. I was too young to eat grass. So I lived on my mother's milk.

There were other young colts in the meadow. I loved to run and play with them!

"You come from a fine family," my mother said. "I hope you do your work well and never learn bad ways."

One day a pack of dogs raced across the field. Many men followed on horseback.

"They are hunting a rabbit," my mother explained.

Suddenly two horses stumbled. Their riders fell head over heels to the ground. A beautiful black horse lay moaning on the grass.

A doctor came. He shook his head. "His leg is broken."

Suddenly a gun went off. *Bang!*

Then all was still. The black horse didn't move.

"I knew that horse," my mother said quietly. "His name was Rob Roy." That was all she said. But she never went to that part of the meadow again.

In time I grew quite handsome. My coat was shiny and black. I had one white foot and a pretty white star on my forehead.

One day Farmer Grey decided it was time to "break me in."

He talked gently and gave me oats.
Then he put a bit into my mouth. I did
not like the taste of it!

Next came the saddle. It was not so
bad.

I learned to wear a harness and a
bridle with blinkers. Now I could see
only straight ahead. Worst of all were
the horseshoes. They made my feet feel
stiff and heavy.

Farmer Grey rode me around the
meadow. How strange it felt! But I was
proud to carry my master.

My mother said, "Some men are kind like our master. Others are not. A horse never knows who will buy him."

I had no idea then, but soon I would leave my first home.

Squire Gordon bought me. Oh, how Mrs. Gordon loved me. She said, "He is such a beauty, with his black coat and sweet face. Let's call him Black Beauty."

John, the groom, stared at me. "Why, he looks just like our old Rob Roy!"

"Didn't you know?" said Squire Gordon. "They had the same mother."

So! Rob Roy was my brother! No wonder my mother was so sad that day.

Horses have no family, I thought. *At least, not after they are sold.*

One night I woke to hear John calling, "Wake up, Black Beauty! Mrs. Gordon is very sick. We must race to get the doctor!"

The air was frosty, and the moon was bright. For seven miles I ran like the wind!

At last we reached the doctor's house in town. "My son has taken my horse," the doctor told John. "May I ride yours?"

John stroked my neck. He knew I was hot and tired. But at last he said, "I guess there is no other way."

So the doctor jumped into the saddle, and off we went!

By the time we got home, I was covered with sweat. My legs were shaking. A young boy named Joe Green led me to the barn.

Joe was new. He did not know what to do. Joe did not put my blanket on me. He gave me cold water. John would have given me something warm to drink.

I lay down and tried to sleep. I could not stop shaking. I wished for John. But he had to walk all the way back from town.

Just before dawn, John came.

"Beauty!" he cried and ran to my side.
He covered me with a warm blanket and
made me something warm to drink.

Even so, I was sick for a long time.

Every day, young Joe Green came to see me. "Poor Black Beauty!" he said. "Did you know you saved Mrs. Gordon's life?"

How glad I was to hear that!

Joe Green worked hard to learn the right way to care for the horses. Soon I got better.

But Mrs. Gordon was never the same. The doctor said she and Squire Gordon must move to a warmer place.

And so I was sold again.

My new owner was an earl. He changed my name to Baron. On the first day a horse named Ginger and I were hooked to a fine carriage.

24

Soon the earl's wife stormed down the steps.

"Pull those horses' heads higher!" she shouted at the groom.

The groom tightened my reins. Oh, how the bit cut my mouth!

But Ginger would not stand for it. She began to fight and kick. The earl was so angry, he sent Ginger away. From then on, I worked alone.

One weekend, a groom named Smith rode me into town on business. It was dark when we headed home. He did not see that I had a loose shoe. Smith whipped me to go faster and faster.

Then my shoe flew off! The rough stones cut into my hoof. Soon the pain was too much to bear, and I stumbled to my knees. Smith fell to the ground.

The next day the doctor came. "This horse will be able to work," he said. "But he will always have those scars."

The earl flew into a rage. "I will not keep a scarred horse in my stables!"

And so I was sold again.

I was lucky. A man with kind eyes bought me. He did not care about the scars. The man's name was Jerry, and he decided to call me Jack.

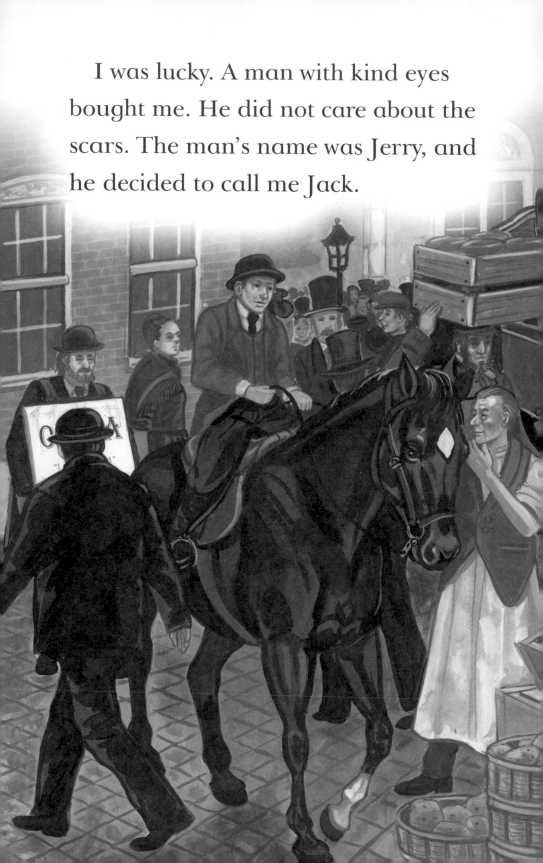

Jerry took me home to London. What a fancy, big city it was! I had never seen so many horses and carriages, or so many people!

Jerry turned down a narrow street of poor-looking houses. Suddenly a door flew open. Out ran his family to greet him.

"What a beauty!" his wife cried.

The children kissed me and petted me.

I thought, *I am going to be happy at last.*

Jerry owned a cab. Rich people in fine clothes paid us to drive them around. It was hard work at first. I was not used to the busy streets of London. But Jerry was a good driver. We made a fine team.

"Good job, Jack!" he would always say.

Soon it was Christmas. But there was
no holiday for us. We took some fine
gentlemen to a party. It was bitter cold,
and we had to wait and wait.

It was long past midnight when we got home. Jerry led me back to my stable. Jerry had a bad cough. But still he took the time to care for me.

After that night, there was no work for days. Jerry was too sick! At last he grew stronger. But the doctor said he could not drive his cab anymore. Jerry and his family made plans to move to the country.

At first I was so excited! But then I learned that Jerry and his family could not take me with them. It broke my heart to say good-bye.

After that I was sold many times. Each time I had a new name. One master was a man named Skinner. He owned cabs.

One evening Skinner picked up a large family. They had so many boxes and bags!

"Oh, Papa!" said the little girl. "This poor horse cannot pull all of our things!"

"Sure he can!" Skinner said.

I was so tired. I had not eaten or rested all day, but I did my best.

We came to a big hill. The load was so heavy.

Skinner pulled hard on the reins.
When I slowed down, he got angry and
whipped me.

   Finally I could not take another step.
I fell to the ground.

I was given ten days to rest. Then Skinner sent me to a horse fair. This time I was put in with the old, broken-down horses.

"This horse has seen better days," an old gentleman said. "He must have been a beauty when he was young."

"Poor thing," said his grandson, Willie. "Can we buy him? I am sure he will grow young in our meadows."

The old man laughed. "You love horses as much as me!" Then he pulled out his purse.

The old man and Willie took me home. They called me Old Crony and took good care of me. I ran free in their meadows.

By spring I was strong enough to pull a small cart.

"You were right, Willie," the old man said. "He is growing young. I know the perfect home for him!"

The next morning I was taken to a nearby house. Three sisters lived there.

The groom was cleaning my face. Suddenly he gasped. "Why, I'd know this white star anywhere. Black Beauty! Don't you know me? I'm Joe Green!"

I stared at him. He looked like young Joe Green—only with black whiskers! Young Joe Green was now a man.

So here I stay. My work is easy, and
Joe is the best of grooms. The ladies
promise never to sell me. Best of all,
everyone calls me by my old name
again. Black Beauty!